The Life and Times
of
CORN

Written and illustrated by Charles Micucci

Houghton Mifflin Books for Children

Houghton Mifflin Harcourt

Boston   New York   2009

For Mom,
Who was born in Mitchell, South Dakota:
Home of the Corn Palace

Houghton Mifflin Books for Children is an imprint of Houghton Mifflin Harcourt Publishing Company.

www.hmhbooks.com

The text of this book is set in Regula Antigua, Adobe Garamond, and Perpetua.
The illustrations are watercolor, gouache, and pencil.

Library of Congress Cataloging-in-Publication Data
Micucci, Charles.
The life and times of corn / written and illustrated by Charles Micucci.
p. cm.
Includes bibliographical references.
ISBN 978-0-618-50751-1
1. Corn—Juvenile literature. I. Title.
SB191.M2M435 2009
633.1'5—dc22
2008040466
Printed in Singapore
TWP 10 9 8 7 6 5 4 3 2 1

Sources:

Bial, Raymond. *Corn Belt Harvest.* Boston: Houghton Mifflin Company, 1991.

Fussell, Betty. *The Story of Corn.* New York: Alfred A. Knopf, 1992.

Hardeman, Nicholas P. *Shucks, Shocks, and Hominy Blocks: Corn as a Way of Life in Pioneer America.* Baton Rouge: Louisiana State University Press, 1981.

Mangelsdorf, Paul C. *Corn: Its Origin, Evolution and Improvement.* Cambridge: Belknap Press of Harvard University, 1974.

Pollan, Michael. *The Omnivore's Dilemma.* New York: Penguin Press, 2006.

Smith, Andrew F. *Popped Culture: A Social History of Popcorn in America.* Washington, D.C.: Smithsonian Institutional Press, 2001.

Weatherwax, Paul. *Indian Corn in Old America.* New York: Macmillan Company, 1954.

———. *The Story of the Maize Plant.* Chicago: University of Chicago Press, 1923.

Acknowledgments:

The author expresses gratitude to the Nebraska Department of Agriculture and the United States Department of Agriculture for their generous
supply of information, and to the librarians at the 42nd Street Library, New York City, for their kind assistance in locating much of the research
    for this book.

For "The Overlooked Discovery," the writings of Paul Weatherwax were very helpful in sifting through facts more than five hundred years old.

For the Native American sections, in addition to Mr. Weatherwax, Betty Fussell's wonderful book and the North American Exhibit at the Museum
    of Natural History, New York City, were helpful in understanding the unique coexistence of a people and a plant.

For the "Life Cycle of Corn," University of Illinois and Ohio State University bulletins prepared to assist corn farmers were very informative.

For general trivia, the author is grateful to the National Corn Growers Association.

My own humble crop of corn provided a hands-on bond between author and subject beyond books. I grew Tom Thumb popcorn in a pot,
    painted mountain corn in a barrel, and a row of hybrid sweet corn near a hedgerow.

Special thanks to my editor, Ann Rider, designer, Rebecca Bond, and my wife, Peggy, for their patience during the five years of researching,
    writing about, and drawing all those corn kernels.

CORNTENTS

THE OVERLOOKED DISCOVERY

When Christopher Columbus returned from his voyages, news spread across Europe of new lands with great treasures. Few people were interested in tales about a tall grass that the natives called maize. The leaders of Europe sought the discovery of gold, not grass.

Little did they know that one day maize, which we call corn, would be planted throughout the world. Today, more than a billion people eat corn.

Columbus barely mentioned corn in his travel log. But some of his men who ate corn with the Arawak tribe reported that it tasted good when boiled, roasted, or baked into bread.

Corn was more than just food to early Native Americans. It was a way of life. Its growing season inspired legends that were passed down many generations.

By the time Columbus arrived in 1492, corn was growing over a 6,000-mile range in North and South America.

North America

South America

actual size

Primitive corn grew in Mexico 7,000 years ago. The first cobs were tiny. As people started cultivating corn, its cobs grew larger.

Columbus found little gold, but that tall grass continues to shine: the annual value of the corn crop in the United States is ten times larger than the gold mined in the country.

50 billion dollars

5 billion dollars

Each year people eat more than 2 million tons of corn, and farm animals crunch and munch more than 160 million tons.

AN A-MAIZE-ING GRAIN

A grain is a grasslike plant that produces seeds that people eat as food. Corn is a grain and so are wheat and oats, but only corn is native to the Americas. The giant of the grains, a corn plant can grow taller than twenty feet, and its roots extend more than six feet.

Corn seeds (kernels) grow together on a cob. Some cobs of corn are more than a foot long and are heavier than a pound.

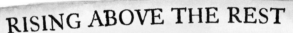

RISING ABOVE THE REST
Corn has unique properties that make it different from other grains.

Corn leaves absorb 97 percent of the plant's nutrition from the air.

Corn yields more seeds per plant than any other grain.

WHEAT
60 seeds

OATS
100 seeds

CORN
800 seeds

Corn cobs are each wrapped in a husk that protects the seeds from wind and rain.

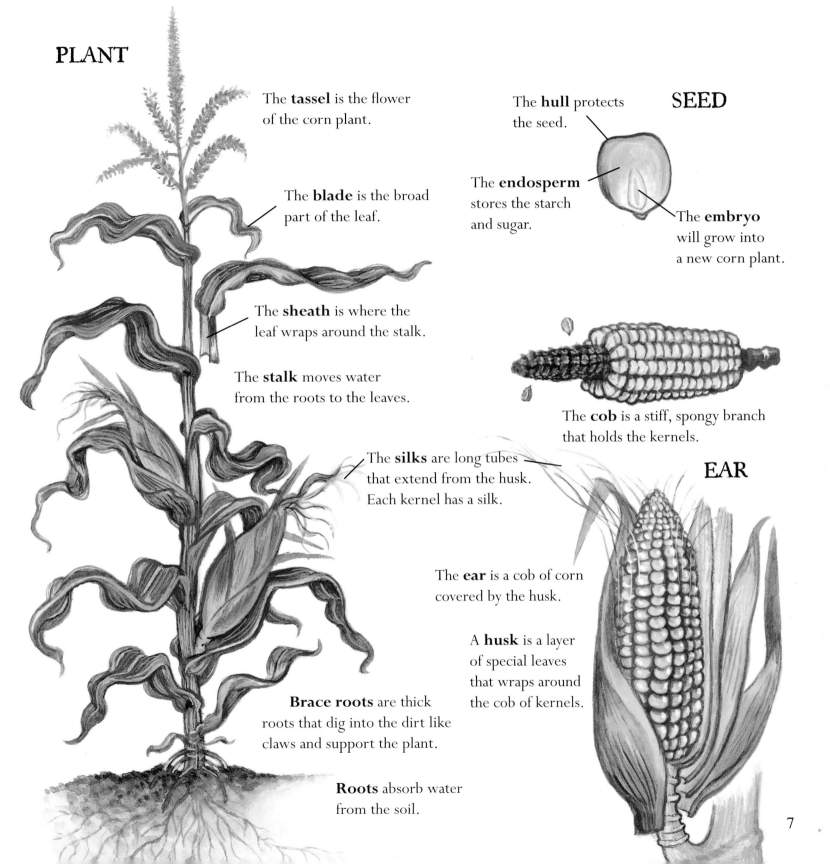

PLANT

The **tassel** is the flower of the corn plant.

The **blade** is the broad part of the leaf.

The **sheath** is where the leaf wraps around the stalk.

The **stalk** moves water from the roots to the leaves.

The **silks** are long tubes that extend from the husk. Each kernel has a silk.

Brace roots are thick roots that dig into the dirt like claws and support the plant.

Roots absorb water from the soil.

SEED

The **hull** protects the seed.

The **endosperm** stores the starch and sugar.

The **embryo** will grow into a new corn plant.

The **cob** is a stiff, spongy branch that holds the kernels.

EAR

The **ear** is a cob of corn covered by the husk.

A **husk** is a layer of special leaves that wraps around the cob of kernels.

FARMERS' FAVORITES

There are more than a thousand kinds of corn, which can be grouped into four major categories: sweet, dent, heirloom, and popcorn.

Each year Americans eat more than three billion ears of sweet corn, some canned, some frozen, and some the fun way . . . fresh off the cob. Celebrated at corn festivals and corn eating contests across the Midwest, sweet corn has been one of America's most popular foods for more than a century.

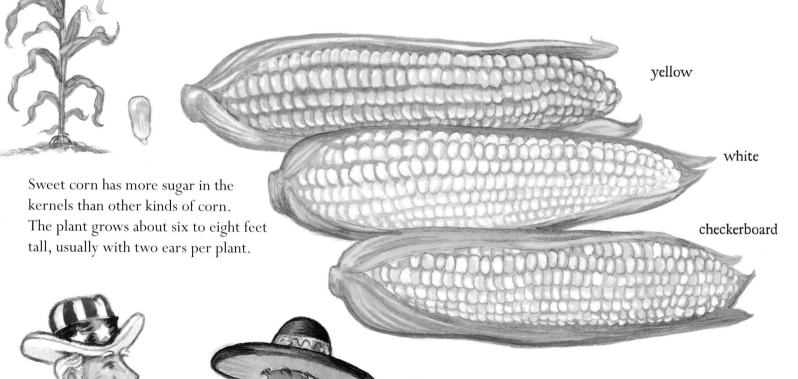

yellow

white

checkerboard

Sweet corn has more sugar in the kernels than other kinds of corn. The plant grows about six to eight feet tall, usually with two ears per plant.

Americans enjoy corn on the cob dripping with butter. Mexican style is rubbed with a lime, or if preferred, "¡Elote!": spread with mayonnaise and sprinkled with chili powder and añejo cheese.

8

For every acre of sweet corn that is planted, farmers plant more than sixty acres of yellow dent corn. About 98 percent of the corn in the United States is yellow dent corn.

Called dent corn because its kernel tops have dents, it is used to feed livestock, as a sweetener, and for industrial products such as ethanol. Farmers prefer dent corn because it produces more kernels per ear than most corns and can be planted close together, yielding larger harvests.

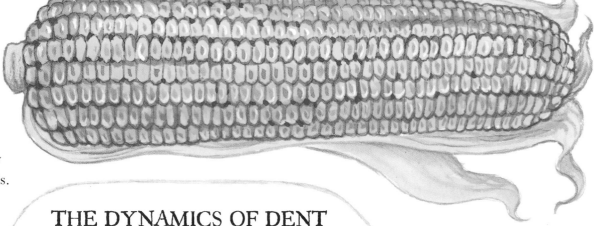

Dent corn plants are about eight feet tall with only one ear per plant. Large ears may have more than 1,200 kernels.

THE DYNAMICS OF DENT

Every fifty pounds of dent corn . . .

that a cow eats,
it gains five pounds

makes enough sweetener
for about 350 glasses of soda

produces two and one-fourth gallons of ethanol, enabling a car to travel from Baltimore to Washington, D.C.

RAINBOWS OF CORN

Corn grows in a wide range of colors. In centuries past, Native Americans cherished ears of corn for their color as well as their size. Corn of many colors is referred to as Indian corn, or heirloom corn. An heirloom is something special that is preserved for future generations.

Heirloom corns have beneficial properties that inspire farmers and gardeners to grow them. Some can survive desert heat; others thrive on high mountains. Many heirloom corns are used as colorful autumn decorations, or ground into flour.

Heirloom corn plants are between three and twenty feet tall. Many have multiple stems and several ears per plant.

Individual corn kernels may have different patterns of color.

| starburst | striped | half and half | speckled | spot |

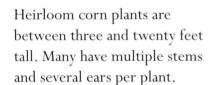

At the end of a harvest, pioneers held a husking bee, where everyone helped husk the corn. If a boy husked a red ear of corn, he was allowed to kiss the girl of his choice.

Jala, from Mexico, has the world's largest ears, more than two feet long.

Granada grows on South American mountains.

Pod corn is the world's oldest corn. Each kernel has its own husk.

Northern flint grows well in cooler climates.

Oxacan green dent from Mexico is made into green tamales.

Hopi pink can grow in the desert.

Blue corn is ground into flour for tortillas and chips.

Mandan red was originally grown on the windy plains of North Dakota.

Maiz morado is made into a soft drink called Chicha Morado in Peru.

Black Aztec is white when first picked, and turns blue-black when it dries.

Painted mountain can survive cold winds and drought.

11

POPPIN' THROUGH THE AGES

Popcorn is America's oldest kind of corn. People living in what is now New Mexico popped corn more than 4,000 years ago.

Popcorn kernels are small and hard and appear to be dry, but in order to pop, they need to contain some moisture. When dampened, kernels older than a thousand years have still popped.

Popcorn plants grow between two and eight feet tall. Each plant may yield six or more ears.

Popcorn also grows in a variety of colors.

Tom Thumb

Mini Pink

Mini Blue

Calico

Dakota Black

Strawberry

2300 B.C.
People popped corn in what is now a bat cave in New Mexico.

A.D. 500
In Peru, the Moche people popped popcorn in clay poppers.

1400s
At some celebrations, Aztec girls wore garlands of popcorn in their hair.

1000
Pueblo Indians, who lived in adobe houses built under cliffs, ate popcorn.

1600s
Some North American tribes cooked popcorn by stirring kernels into sand that had been heated by a campfire.

HOW POPCORN POPS

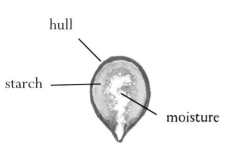

hull

starch

moisture

When a kernel is heated, moisture within the kernel turns into steam.

Pressure builds. The starch melts into a gel. Suddenly, the hull can't hold it . . .

POP!

The kernel explodes inside out.

The starch instantly dries while inflating forty times its original size. The steam spreads popcorn aroma into the air.

1840s
Pioneers cooked popcorn in square wire mesh baskets.

1890s
Sidewalk vendors in Chicago cooked popcorn with steam-powered poppers.

1912
People started munching popcorn at the movies.

1945
Percy Spencer, a scientist, invented microwave popcorn while experimenting with microwave energy.

1772
Joseph Cooper, a New Jersey farmer, grew popcorn with eight to ten ears per plant.

2000s
Each year Americans eat more than fifty quarts of popcorn per person.

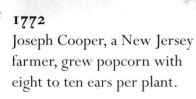

GROWING TO THE SUN

Corn plants grow to maturity in about four months. During the first two months, the plant produces leaves, which absorb energy from the sun and carbon from the air. Down below, the roots absorb water from the dirt. Together, these elements make the plant grow taller. Farmers call this time the vegetative stage.

PLANTING CORN

A gardener uses a stick to make a hole, plants a few seeds, then fills in the dirt with a trowel.

OR

A farmer drives a tractor that drills several holes and drops in the seed. Then wheels fill the holes in with dirt.

A kernel of corn is planted one to four inches deep.

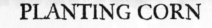

May 1   May 9   May 20   June 1   June 13

When a corn seed first sprouts, the faster-growing root shoots down. Soon after, the beginnings of a stalk come up.

14

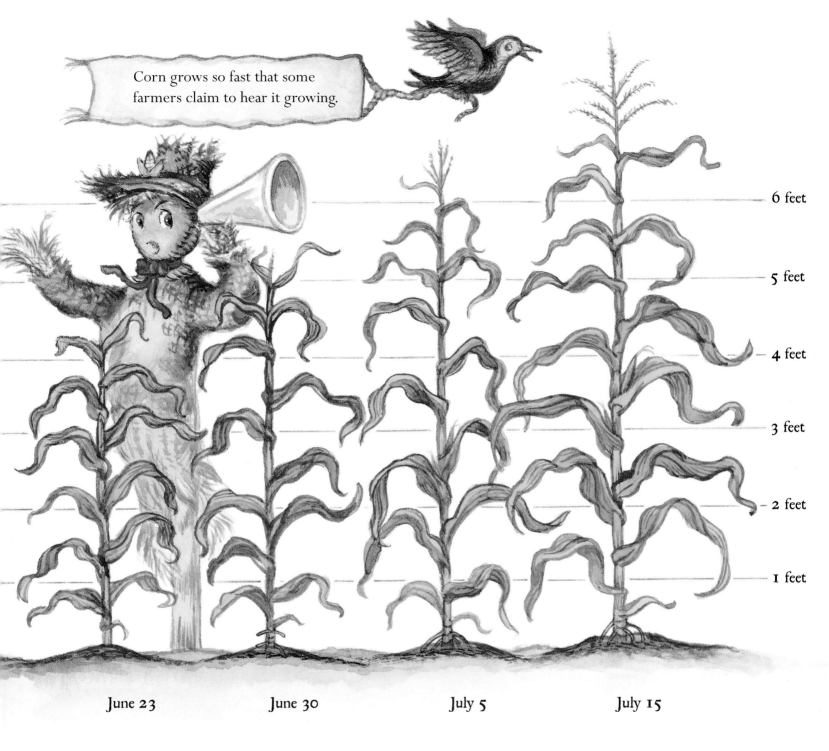

Corn grows so fast that some farmers claim to hear it growing.

6 feet

5 feet

4 feet

3 feet

2 feet

1 feet

June 23

June 30

July 5

July 15

Brace roots extend as the plant prepares for the weight of the ears.

The tassel sprouts up, and now the plant is ready for the next phase: producing corn.

15

TREASURE IN THE WIND

During the last two months, a corn plant does not grow many more leaves, or grow much taller. Instead, it pushes forth ear buds fluffed with silks. Farmers call this time the reproductive phase.

In the morning, the tassel releases tiny grains of pollen. The wind blows the pollen across the cornfield.

As pollen drifts across the plants, it sticks to the silks. Now kernels of corn begin to grow.

END OF JULY

After the kernels start to grow, the silks darken. A farmer can look on his fields and tell that corn is on its way by the change of color.

During the last couple of weeks, the plant absorbs more than half its total intake of water. The plant converts this water to grow big ears of corn.

MID-AUGUST

Sweet corn is harvested when the plant is still green and the kernels are juicy and have a high sugar content.

SEPTEMBER–OCTOBER

Dent corn is harvested when the plant is straw colored. The kernels are dry and the sugar has turned to starch, which fattens cattle and pigs.

HARVESTING CORN

On farms, some sweet and heirloom corn is still picked by hand. Dent corn and popcorn are harvested by combines. Combines are large tractors that not only pick the corn but also husk and shell it.

Some sweet corn is picked after midnight so the corn is cooler and stays fresh longer.

THREE STEPS TO HARVESTING CORN

Picking
The ear of corn is removed by twisting it down and away from the stalk.

Husking
The husk is peeled away from the ear of corn.

Shelling
The kernels are knocked off the cob.

hopper

HARVESTING BY COMBINE

The corn head knocks down the corn plant and snaps the ear from the plant. Inside, wheels husk and shell the corn. Then the kernels are blown into a hopper, and the husks, leaves, and stalks are dropped into the ground.

husks, leaves,
and stalks

corn head

auger

When the hopper is full, the combine unloads the corn into a truck, through a tube called an auger.

The truck delivers the corn to a grain elevator, where it is weighed and stored until a train transports the corn to a processing facility. There the kernels are made into a variety of products.

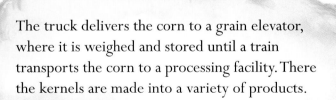

19

BUSHELS OF CORN

Each year farmers around the world harvest more than thirty-one billion bushels of corn. More than 40 percent of it, about thirteen billion bushels, is harvested in the United States. Each bushel weighs fifty-six pounds and contains kernels from about ninety-one cobs.

LEADING CORN AREAS

(Each bushel equals one billion bushels.)

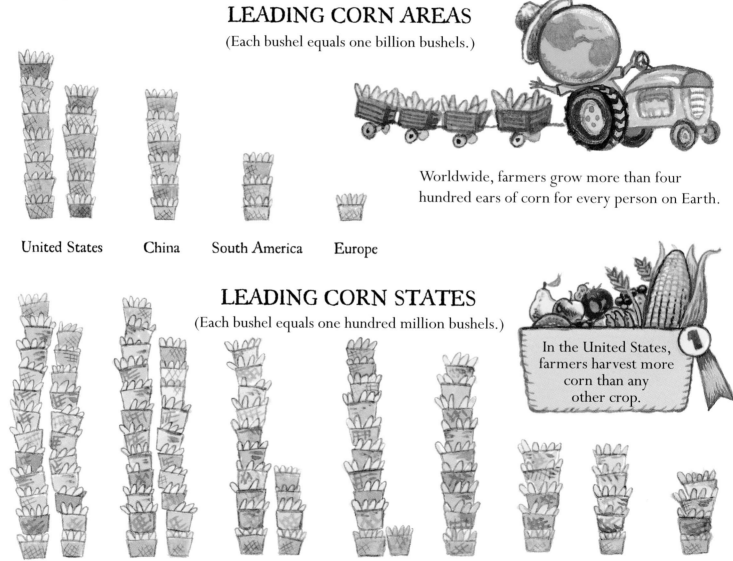

United States   China   South America   Europe

Worldwide, farmers grow more than four hundred ears of corn for every person on Earth.

LEADING CORN STATES

(Each bushel equals one hundred million bushels.)

In the United States, farmers harvest more corn than any other crop.

Iowa   Illinois   Nebraska   Minnesota   Indiana   South Dakota   Ohio   Kansas

THEN AND NOW

Improved farming techniques have increased corn harvests in the United States.

Seed

Before the 1920s, many corn plants fell over, some wouldn't grow tall, and others produced ears with few kernels.

Today, most farmers plant hybrid corn seed. Hybrid seed produces almost identical plants that grow tall and sturdy and produce full ears of corn.

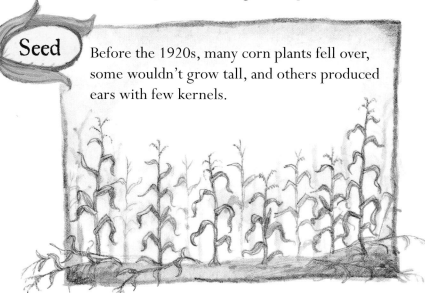

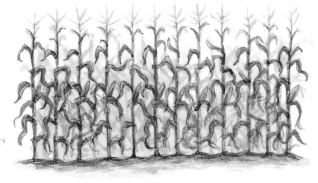

Average yield per farm = 20 bushels an acre

Average yield per farm = 165 bushels an acre

Harvesting

At the turn of the century, picking corn from one plant at a time was hard work.

Today, a large combine can pick corn from twelve corn plants at the same time.

40 bushels per day

40 bushels per minute

A CORNUCOPIA OF USES

Corn is used in more products than any other grain. Most corn is fed to livestock, made into sweeteners, or distilled into ethanol, a fuel for cars. About one-fourth of all supermarket items contain some form of corn.

USES FOR THE KERNEL

livestock feed for cattle, pigs, turkeys, chickens, and fish

sweetener for soda, juice, cakes, cookies, and candy

fresh on the cob

canned

frozen

creamed

cornmeal

cereal

corn syrup

margarine

mayonnaise

salad dressing

cooking oil

Corn flakes were created in 1898 by the Kellogg brothers. Millions of bowls of corn flakes are eaten each day.

paint

ink

artificial silk

plastics

garbage bags

batteries

laundry starch

disposable diapers

baby powder

soap

MAKING THINGS GO

Ethanol has been fueling cars for more than one hundred years. Henry Ford's first car, the 1896 Quadricycle, ran on ethanol. Ethanol made from corn is a renewable resource: new corn can be planted each year. Kernels, stalks, and cobs can be made into ethanol.

STALKS

maizolith
(rubber substitute)

paper

HUSKS AND LEAVES

corn husk
dolls

doormats

COBS

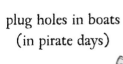

processed into fertilizer

plug holes in boats
(in pirate days)

A MENU OF MAIZE

Johnny cake

fritter

Corn is a versatile food that has inspired cooks for centuries. Dried corn can be ground into flour for baking. Fresh corn can be boiled, fried, or roasted. Corn is a source of carbohydrates, which provide us with energy.

muffin

hush puppy

corn dog

Corn bread has a sweet taste that is enjoyed in a variety of forms, including muffins and loaves. **Johnny cakes** are a nickname for corn bread pancakes. **Fritters** are smaller and thicker, but just as tasty. Fried corn dough balls, called **hush puppies,** are served at southern barbecues. **Corn dogs,** hot dogs cooked in corn flour batter on sticks, are big hits at amusement parks.

Tortillas, flattened cornmeal baked on a griddle, are the primary breads in Mexico. They are used to wrap tacos.

Corn chips are miniature fried tortillas, first sold in a humble Texas café. Today there are more than one hundred kinds, in many flavors.

Tamales are corn dough filled with beans or other ingredients and steamed in a corn husk; sometimes sold by street vendors.

Succotash is a casserole of corn, beans, and squash, originally cooked by Native Americans from the northeast United States.

Baby corn is listed in many Chinese recipes. The soft ears of corn are eaten whole: kernels and cobs.

Polenta is cornmeal boiled in water or baked in the oven. Once eaten by peasants, it's now served at fine Italian restaurants.

Parched corn, dry roasted kernels, was eaten as a snack by Indian hunters while hiking through the woods.

Piki, ground blue corn roasted into large sheets, has been eaten by the Hopi people of Arizona for more than a thousand years.

Corn chowder makes a warm and hearty meal on a cool autumn evening.

Grits are ground cornmeal boiled into porridge. They are a popular breakfast cereal in the American South.

Hasty pudding, made from grated corn, maple syrup, and milk, was a common food during the early days of America.

Yankee Doodle
Early American verse

Father and I went down to camp,
And there was Captain Gooding,
And there we saw the men and boys,
As thick as hasty pudding.

Yankee Doodle keep it up,
Yankee Doodle dandy,
Mind the music and the step
And with the girls be handy!

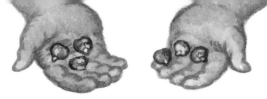

GUIDING HANDS

gold sculpture
Peru

Corn is one of agriculture's great mysteries. It has never been found growing in the wild, because its seeds need to be broken out of the husk in order to grow into corn bearing plants. If people did not grow corn every year, it would soon go extinct.

   The first people to plant corn were the Native Americans. They needed corn for food, and corn needed them for its existence. Native Americans planted corn with their hands, and they revered it with their hearts.

clay bottle
Mexico

Native Americans expressed their love of corn in their art and crafts.

clay water pot
Peru

cliff painting
New Mexico

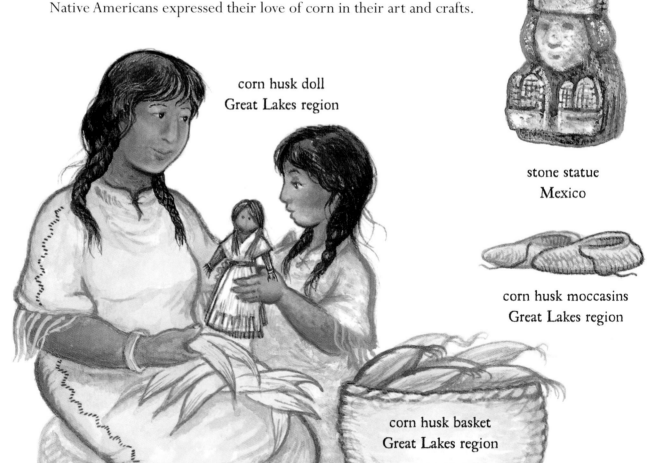

corn husk doll
Great Lakes region

stone statue
Mexico

corn husk moccasins
Great Lakes region

corn husk basket
Great Lakes region

THE THREE SISTERS

How corn, beans, and squash were planted
five hundred years ago.

Several corn seeds
were planted in a
hill of dirt.

When the plants
were about three
hands high, beans
were planted in the
hills, and squash
in between.

The beans grew
up the stalk, and
squash blocked the
growth of weeds.

After nature's work
was done, it was time
to harvest the corn,
beans, and squash.

Beneath the setting sun, the tribe gave thanks
for the three sisters: corn, beans, and squash.

SHARING CORN CULTURE

When European settlers sailed to America, they were greeted by an unfriendly land of swarming mosquitoes in the summer and bone-chilling bleakness in the winter.

Often, they planted seeds from Europe, only to watch them wither away and die. Native Americans showed the settlers how to grow corn, which thrived in their adopted land.

In the spring of 1621, Squanto, a Wampanoag native, showed Pilgrims from Massachusetts how to fertilize corn by planting corn seeds with fish.

That fall the Pilgrims invited Squanto and some Wampanoags over for a Thanksgiving feast, which historians believe included deer, fish, duck, geese, wild turkey, beans, squash, berries, and corn.

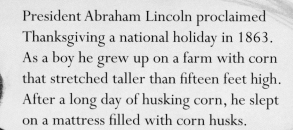

Two years earlier, settlers in Virginia celebrated their first Thanksgiving. Some historians believe that bacon, peas, and unsweetened cornmeal cakes made up their humble meal of gratitude.

President Abraham Lincoln proclaimed Thanksgiving a national holiday in 1863. As a boy he grew up on a farm with corn that stretched taller than fifteen feet high. After a long day of husking corn, he slept on a mattress filled with corn husks.

ADOPTING NATIVE CORN CULTURE

Native **Settler**

Natives and settlers stored corn in corncribs, built on stilts, which protected the corn from floods.

Natives showed settlers how to knock kernels off the cob with seashells. The term "shelling corn" is still used.

Natives and settlers tied corn plants together in bundles called "shocks."

PROTECTING THE HARVEST FROM BIRDS

Virginia tribes posted men in guard huts that stood above the cornfield. Guards were on duty all day and night.

Virginia colonists posted guards on platforms with strings tied to corn plants. When the guard pulled the string and the plants moved, the birds flew away.

Settlers from England made "shoy hoys" to scare away birds, just as their ancestors had since the 1300s. In America, many of the birds they wanted to scare were crows, so they renamed it the "scarecrow."

CORN COUNTRY

Today, corn is grown in every state. Its fields cover one-fourth of America's cropland, an area of about 125,000 square miles. If "Corn" were a separate state, it would be the fifth-largest state in America.

Five Largest States
if Corn were a state

1. Alaska: 663,267 square miles
2. Texas: 268,581 square miles
3. California: 163,696 square miles
4. Montana: 147,042 square miles
5. Corn: 125,000 square miles

The world's only corn palace, in Mitchell, South Dakota, is decorated with thousands of ears of corn.

Henry Wallace, from Iowa, was a corn expert who served as vice president from 1941–45 for Franklin D. Roosevelt.

Nebraska is nicknamed "the Corn Husker State." Their college football team is called the Corn Huskers.

Hopi farmers place stones near corn seedlings to block hot desert winds.

During the 1930s, corn husking contests were broadcast over the radio.

Texas tops the country in cattle. Across America, more than sixty million cattle feed on corn.

California is the leading dairy state. Many dairy cattle eat corn silage, chopped corn plants.

World's Oldest Popcorn New Mexico 2300 B.C.

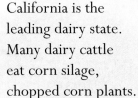

Iowa, Illinois, Nebraska, Indiana, Minnesota, Ohio, Kansas, South Dakota, Missouri, Wisconsin, Michigan, and Kentucky make up the "Corn Belt": the world's largest corn-growing area.

In the 1700s and 1800s, water-powered mills ground corn into flour so pioneers could make corn bread.

During the Revolutionary War, the Onedia people delivered corn to George Washington's troops at Valley Forge.

World's Largest Popcorn Ball Peekskill, New York 12 feet across 1981

In 2007, cars that raced at the Indy 500 ran on ethanol.

Cahokia Mounds, a city of 20,000 people, flourished in southern Illinois 1,000 years ago by growing corn and other foods.

"Hogging down!" is a harvesting process in which farmers let their pigs tear down the stalks and gobble corn. Oink-oink!

In 1983, Barbara McClintock, from Cold Spring Harbor, New York, was awarded a Nobel Prize for her research on how genes determine the color of corn kernels.

Pocahontas was kidnapped in 1613, and held for a ransom of a boat full of corn.

Arkansas raises more chickens than any other state. In the United States nearly four billion chickens eat corn.

Florida grows more sweet corn than any other state. Its warm climate allows a longer growing season.

N
W   E
S

America is the world's greatest corn exporter. Each year the United States ships more than 1.7 billion bushels of corn to other countries.

In Native American culture, different colors of corn symbolize the four prime directions.

31

Corn has been planted across America for centuries because of its abundant yield and its many useful purposes. Now the future of corn is in the hands of our farmers and gardeners. Each time they reach for a tassel or peel back a husk, they add new chapters to the life and times of corn.

A-MAIZE-ING SEASONAL ACTIVITIES

SUMMER: CORN FESTIVALS
To celebrate corn, communities throw parties of music, games, and plenty of corn.

AUTUMN: CORN MAZES
Farmers open up their fields as living puzzles with people wandering inside.

WINTER: STRINGS OF POPCORN
For more than a hundred years, people have decorated Christmas trees with popcorn.

In the late 1890s and early 1900s, some seed catalogues were decorated with simple jokes that farmers called "corn jokes." In the 1930s, musicians popularized the word "corny" to describe anything old fashioned or sentimental.

Corn took a giant leap in 1969, when the *Apollo 11* astronauts ate corn flakes on their way to the moon. Fasten your seat belts — corn is out of this world!